1.3
6

D0501208

A NOTE TO PARENTS

Young children can be overwhelmed by their emotions--often because they don't understand and can't express what they are feeling. This, in turn, can frustrate parents. How can you help your child deal with a problem if the two of you don't even share a common vocabulary?

Welcome to **HOW I FEEL**--a series of books designed to bridge this communication gap. With simple text, lively illustrations, and an interactive format, each book describes familiar situations to help children recognize a particular emotion. It gives them a vocabulary to talk about what they're feeling, and it offers practical suggestions for dealing with those feelings.

Each time you read this book with your child you can reinforce the message with one of the following activities:

- Ask your child to make up a story about a little boy or girl who is acting silly.

- Make a list together of silly words--real or imaginary.

- Act out situations in which it's okay to be silly, and situations in which it's not.

- Explore different emotions using the Make-a-Face activity card and reuseable stickers included with this book.

I hope you both enjoy the **HOW I FEEL** series, and that it will help your child take the first steps toward understanding emotions.

Marcia Leonard

Executive Producers, JOHN CHRISTIANSON and RON BERRY
Art Design, GARY CURRANT
Layout Design, CURRANT DESIGN GROUP and BEST IMPRESSION GRAPHICS

HOW i FEEL

SILLY

by Marcia Leonard
illustrated by Bartholomew

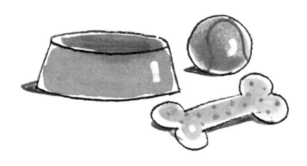

This little girl is pretending
to be a puppy.
She likes being silly.

These kids like being silly, too.
They're having a good time
clowning around outside.

When this little boy feels silly,
he makes funny faces.

Have you ever done that?
Can you make a face that looks silly?

When these little girls feel silly,
they make funny sounds.

Can you make up silly words, too?

There are times when it's okay to be silly, and times when it's not.

Does this look like a good time to be silly?

There are places where it's good to be silly,
and places where it's not.

Do you think this is a good place?

If you are silly at the wrong time or place,
you might bother other people.

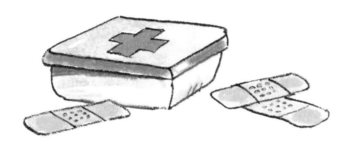

And if your silliness gets too wild,
someone might even get hurt.

You can have a loud and bouncy,
giggly good time when you feel silly.

But after a while,
it's good to take time out
for some quieter fun.

MAKE-A-FACE
Instructions

Use this Make-a-Face activity to help your child identify and express a variety of emotions. Gently remove the page of reusable stickers from the center of this book. Let your child use the stickers to make faces on the blank card. Then talk about the faces. Are they silly, scared or angry? It's easy for your child to Make-a-Face--and fun too!